Oh Mylanta!

They said,

"There's No Santa!"

Published by Mindstir Media, LLC
45 Lafayette Rd | Suite 181| North Hampton, NH 03862 | USA
1.800.767.0531 | www.mindstirmedia.com

Printed in the United States of America
ISBN-13: 978-1-7329482-9-7
Library of Congress Control Number: 2018913456

Oh Mylanta!

They said,
"There's No Santa!"

BY RYAN D. GAUDREAU

ILLUSTRATED BY EILEEN MAILHOT

MINDSTIR MEDIA

DEDICATION

This book is dedicated to my twin nephews:

Joshua Paul & Nicholas Ryan

May all of your many Christmases be rich with love.

Last Christmas was a wonderful time;
celebrated with family, love, music, and rhyme.

Christmas time is Suzy and Johnny's favorite season.
They love the warmth, cheer, and presents as reason!

They behave in school and always try to be nice.
They know Santa is watching, checking them twice.

Even when Johnny would be mean to his sister,
their Mom would say, "Hey! Be nice to her mister!"

One day at school someone had said,
"There is no Santa! No man in red!"

Suzy and Johnny were so very sad.
Why would he say that? It made them so mad!

So Suzy and Johnny asked their parents that day.
There had to be a Santa! There had to be a way!

Later that night when they were all tucked in,
their Mom looked at them with a big wide grin.

She said, "No matter what you might hear at
school or on the bus,
there is a Santa. He lives within us.

For the rest of your life he'll be on your shoulder,
watching out for you as you get older.

So when I am not with you nor even your Dad,
you still must behave and do nothing bad.

It is not for the presents why you must be good.
It is because we have loved you;
that's why you should.

So as long as I love you, Santa is real.
It's not something you see. It's something you feel."

Although Suzy and Johnny were somewhat confused,
their Mom just smiled and looked quite amused.

So as they drifted off dreaming of sugar-plum fairies,
they could hear the sweet songs of morning canaries.

And just out the window sat a lonesome white dove,
not a symbol of Christmas, but a symbol of love.

CPSIA information can be obtained at www.ICGtesting.com
Printed in the USA
BVIW122101060119
537129BV00044B/582